Ellen B. Senisi

Berry Smudges and Leaf Prints

Finding and Making Colors from Nature

DUTTON CHILDREN'S BOOKS • NEW YORK

Thinking About Colors

Think of your favorite place outside. Now imagine that place without color—any color at all. Is it still beautiful or interesting? In a colorless world, would you notice flowers to pick or a nice rock to take home? Would you even want to if everything looked the same? If you are starting to think that color is a very important part of what attracts you to a special place, you're right.

Color affects us. It touches our feelings. A bright red sunset can thrill us. A blue lake can make us feel peaceful. A gray sky might make us feel worried, sad, or tired.

Color can make something seem beautiful or ugly to us. The clothes you chose today probably have colors that you like a lot, colors that look good to you. Almost everyone has a favorite and a least favorite color.

Often, in our color choices, we are trying to tell others something about ourselves—about how we feel, what we like, or what group we belong to (think of team colors or the colors of the flag). The expressiveness of color makes it a very important part of art, fashion, and decoration.

Using color to communicate is so important to people that even before there were crayons, pencils, paints, or makeup, our ancestors had figured out other ways to get color—from nature.

Have you ever noticed that your fingers turn yellow after plucking buttercups? Or red after picking berries? Do your parents wish you wouldn't come home with grass stains on your clothes? Scientists think these same kinds of color accidents happened to people thousands of years ago, too. These early humans looked twice at their stained fingers and began experimenting to find ways to gather and use color.

Cave dwellers in prehistoric Europe painted murals on the walls of their dark homes with mud and ocher, a red or yellow color made from iron ore. The ancient Egyptians created their own makeup from natural sources. They ground malachite, a green ore, into eye shadow and charcoal and certain black ores into eyeliner. The Pacific Islanders of Micronesia made orange body paint from a mixture of coconut oil and a spice called turmeric.

You, too, can use colors from nature just as people did long ago, and as some artists and craftspeople still do today. This book is a celebration of the colors of the natural world and a guide to homemade coloring. All the materials you will need for the many projects in this book can be found in yards, parks, gardens, or garden and grocery stores.

Some projects can be done only at certain times of the year. In some cases, you may be able to buy the ingredients year-round at a food store, but in others, you (like your ancestors) will just have to wait for the right season.

Whether you want to create colors or just admire them, this book will start you on the path to discovering the colors of nature. Turn the pages and then take a walk outside.

Red

Red is an attention-getting color. There is so much green in nature—leaves, grass, stalks—that red really stands out. Red flowers, berries, and fruits seem to say "Look at me!" And we do. So do insects and animals.

That shiny red apple, so easy to spot against the leaves of the tree, is part of the plant's way of attracting a passing animal. Why? The apple has seeds inside. And to grow, the seeds need soil and their own patch of sunlight, away from the shade of the parent tree. Without wings or legs, the seeds need some other transportation. When a hungry creature notices the bright red fruit, the seed holder, it eats the apple, seeds and all. Eventually the satisfied diner flies or wanders away from the tree. The seeds, which are very hard, pass through the creature undigested. If they are dropped on a good spot of ground, they may grow into new trees.

So red wants attention and gets it. Looking at red actually makes people's hearts beat faster! Maybe that's why we associate it with love (think of the color of valentines) and emergencies (many fire engines are red). Red is the color of excitement and happiness, but also danger and courage. Superman's cape is red, after all. Some people say they see red when they are angry. Red is a strong color and matches strong actions and feelings.

Berry Smudges

You can use red berries to make red and pink paints and stains. (Pink is "light red.") As you do these and other activities in the book, you will find that some colored objects in nature will make the color they are, but others will make a different one. Be prepared for surprises.

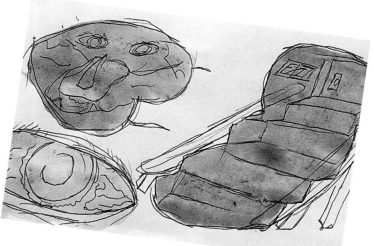

What you are making:
Pictures made with berry juice, smudged on paper

Materials:
- fresh or frozen raspberries
- a plate
- paper
- a pencil or pen

How to do it:
- Choose a berry to smudge with and put it on a small plate. (You really need only one berry to do this project, which means you should have plenty left over to nibble as you work. If you plan to nibble, rinse off fresh berries first.)

- Mush your finger in the berry, then use your finger to smear the juice on the paper.

- Look at your smudge carefully and see if the shape reminds you of anything—a horse, a boat, an umbrella, anything.

- Use your pencil or pen to fill out the drawing so everyone else can see what you saw in your smudge.

For more fun: Experiment with other kinds of berries. Some will smear colors; others will not.

Warning: If you've picked the berries yourself, check with a parent before using or eating them. Some berries are poisonous.

Berry Nice Wrapping Paper

What you are making:
Gift wrap decorated with potato prints

Materials:
- red natural dye (see pages 34–35)
- a rectangular pan (disposable)
- cornstarch
- a potato
- a kitchen knife (and a grown-up to help you use it)
- cookie cutters
- a large sheet of plain paper

How to do it:
- Pour dye into pan.
- Add cornstarch a teaspoon at a time until the dye thickens into a paint. (Dye by itself is too watery to make a good print. You'll notice that the white cornstarch turns the liquid from red to pink.)

- Ask a grown-up to cut a potato in half.
- Choose a cookie cutter and press it into the cut side of a potato half.
- Ask the grown-up helping you to cut away the potato around the outside of the cookie cutter as shown.
- Carefully remove the cookie cutter from your potato. Your stamp is ready.
- Dip your stamp in the paint and press it on your paper. Repeat until your paper is decorated to your liking. (Note: You may want to test your stamp on scrap paper first to see how much paint you need to make a complete shape.)

You can also stamp directly on paper with fresh or frozen strawberries or raspberries. Try decorating stationery or wrapping paper with berries.

Dear Mom,
I really think you take very good care of me. I am very Lucky to have a Mom like you. Love Chandler

7

Blue

Blue is one of nature's biggest colors. You can see across miles of blue ocean and look up into an endless blue sky. But blue is also found in small things. Some birds, flowers, butterflies, berries, and fruits are blue. There are also a few blue rocks and minerals.

Have you ever wondered why water in a lake or ocean is often blue, while the water that comes from a faucet is clear? Water is like glass. It is clear, but its surface reflects the colors around it. Water only appears blue when it is reflecting the blue of the sky. When the sky is gray or sunset red, the water below will look gray or red also.

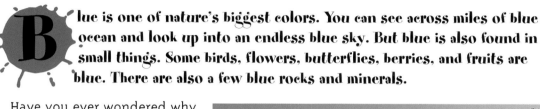

Blue is a restful color. It can remind us of the calmness of a lake or pond and the dreaminess of a clear summer day. People often choose it for bedroom or hospital walls. But the bigness of blue can make people feel alone and sad. When we feel that way, we say we have "the blues."

A Big Blue Picture

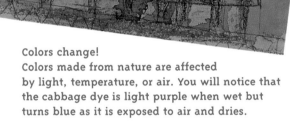

Painting a big blue sky or ocean is easy with a blue wash. (Believe it or not, it's made from red cabbage, which isn't blue at all.) And you can capture the beauty of small blue flowers in a sun catcher for your school or bedroom window.

What you are making:
A drawing with blue wash brushed over it

Materials:
* paper
* crayons, a permanent marker, and/or a black pen
* blue natural dye (see pages 34–35)
* a paintbrush

Colors change!
Colors made from nature are affected by light, temperature, or air. You will notice that the cabbage dye is light purple when wet but turns blue as it is exposed to air and dries.

How to do it:
● Make a drawing using crayons, a permanent marker, and/or a pen.

● Brush blue dye over your drawing. (A light color brushed over a drawing is called a wash. You can use any of the dyes on pages 34–35 as a wash.)

A Sun Catcher

What you are making:
A sun catcher to hang in a window

Materials:
- fresh or pressed* blue flowers
- wax paper
- an iron (and a grown-up to help you use it)
- scissors
- clear tape or contact paper
- a pencil
- thread

How to do it:
- Gather fresh or pressed* flowers. (Pressed flowers are easier to use and their color will last longer. Fresh wildflowers wilt quickly, so pick them just before using. Chicory, a common roadside flower, was used here.)
- Arrange flowers in a design on a piece of wax paper. Paper should be about 6 to 8 inches long.
- Cover the flowers with a second piece of wax paper about the same size.
- Ask an adult to press the pieces of paper together with a hot iron. If you are using pressed flowers, iron around them. If using fresh flowers, iron lightly through a cloth to flatten.
- Cut the wax paper into the shape you want for your sun catcher.
- Seal the edges with tape or clear contact paper.
- Poke a hole with a pencil through the top of the catcher and string some thread through it.
- Hang your sun catcher in a window.

*You can press flowers by placing them between sheets of wax paper and putting them under a heavy pile of books for one week. For more information, see note about flower preservation on page 22.

Yellow

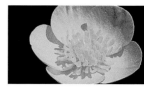

Yellow is the color of the sun, which lights all of nature. You can find yellow on some birds, fish, and butterflies. It is also the color of many flowers, fruits, and vegetables. Like red, it attracts animals and insects.

A bee, which uses a flower's nectar to make food, knows yellow can mean mealtime. It will fly right past a plant's green leaves to the yellow petals of its blossom. As the bee collects nectar, some of the flower's pollen—the powdery stuff at the center of the bloom—clings to the insect's legs and body. The pollen travels with the bee to a new flower, where it may be rubbed off again. Pollen taken from one flower to another helps new plants grow.

As the color of sunshine and many spring flowers, yellow represents beginnings—the beginning of a new day and of spring, the growing season. It is often thought of as a hopeful, happy color. But yellow is also the color of fire, so it can make us think of danger. Caution signs on curving roads or at busy intersections are yellow. School buses are, too, warning drivers not to speed by when students are getting on or off.

Yellow, like all colors, has some negative meanings. It can be the color of cowards—as in "he's yellow"—and of sickness. Old sailing ships would raise a yellow warning flag if they had someone with a contagious illness onboard.

A Yellow Nature Weaving

Do you collect a lot of interesting things when you walk outside? Now you can weave them into a bright yellow hanging for your bedroom or classroom.

What you are making:

A nature weaving to hang on your wall

Materials:

- a four-ounce skein of undyed yarn
- yellow natural dye (see pages 34–35)
- a grown-up to help you get started
- a stick or dowel about 9 to 12 inches long
- a support to tie your weaving to as you work, such as a chair back, coatrack, or tree branch
- scissors
- a yarn needle or a crochet hook
- a wide-toothed comb or pick
- a ruler
- natural objects to weave into the yarn, such as a feather, a short stick, a flower, a leaf, or herbs. (Herbs are nice to use because they make your artwork smell as good as it looks.)

How to do it:

- Dye yarn yellow, following the instructions on pages 34–35. Allow yarn to dry thoroughly before using.

- Ask a grown-up to help you start the weaving.

- To create the warp (the up and down part of a weaving), he or she should tie one end of the yarn to the center of the stick and then loop the yarn loosely around the chair back or whatever support is being used. (Note that you will need to slip your weaving off the top or end of the support when it's finished.) There should be about 10 to 12 inches of yarn between the knot and the support. Bring the yarn back to the stick and, next to the first knot, attach the yarn again with two slipknots or by winding the yarn around the stick twice.

- Repeat looping process, alternating sides of the stick, until there are about 14 warp yarns whose knots take up about 6 to 8 inches on the stick. Cut off and tie the last loop securely.

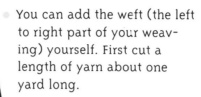

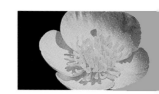

- You can add the weft (the left to right part of your weaving) yourself. First cut a length of yarn about one yard long.

- Use a yarn needle or a crochet hook to weave that piece of yarn under the first warp string, over the second, under the third, over the fourth, etc.

- Pull the yarn almost all the way through, leaving just two inches to be tied later.

- Repeat the weaving process with the same piece of yarn, going back through the other way. This time, do the opposite—if you ended the last step by going under a yarn strand, start by going over that strand, under the next, etc.

- Repeat four or five times. You can use the comb or pick to push the weft strings down as you work.

- To add a natural object, begin by weaving in a ruler instead of the yarn. Turn the ruler to create a space. Place the natural object in the space and gently pull the ruler out. Weave at least 3 to 4 more rows of yarn before adding another natural object.

- Continue to weave until you don't have enough weft yarn to weave through again. Knot the loose ends of the yarn and tuck them into the weaving.

- Slip your weaving off the support and tie a short piece of yarn to the top of it for hanging.

Green

Sometimes it seems as if green is nature's favorite color. Green is the color of the grass, trees, bushes, and other plants that surround us. So much of our food comes from plants that we think of green as the color of life and growing.

If you have ever looked very closely at the green plant world, you may have noticed the small creatures that live and hide there. Many frogs, snakes, lizards, and insects are hard to see because their green color helps them blend into their surroundings. This keeps them safe from animals that might eat them. So green is also the color of hiding, or camouflage. Soldiers fighting in the woods often wear green so they won't be noticed by the enemy.

Many people are afraid of snakes, lizards, and other green hiding creatures. Maybe that is why imaginary monsters like dragons and horror-movie creatures are often green.

Green, which is actually a mixture of calm blue and sunny yellow, is also a restful color. Early craftsmen who strained their eyes doing close work, like engraving, would keep a clear green jewel to look through to give their eyes a rest.

Great Green Leaf Prints

Sometimes in winter, the feeling of green and growing is far away. You can make a collage to hang on the wall to remind you of spring. Or write about a favorite scene or object from nature with homemade green ink.

What you are making:

A collage of green leaves, stems, and vines, hammered onto plain cloth

Materials:

- an assortment of green leaves, stems, and vines
- unbleached muslin cloth
- scrap pieces of the same cloth
- tape
- wax paper
- a hammer

How to do it:

- Find a sturdy worktable or a sidewalk to work on.
- Choose leaves, stems, and vines. (You will find that thick, sturdy, dark green leaves usually work best. Be sure to use green stems instead of brown, woody ones. The green shoots of some vines will add graceful, curving lines to your collage.)
- Test your leaves on the scrap pieces of cloth. Some kinds will work well and some won't. Place the top, or shiny side, of the leaves face up and the bottom, or dull side, face down, touching the cloth. Use a few pieces of tape to hold them in place.
- Put wax paper over the leaves and hammer away. (Hammer evenly and hard, going over and over every part of the leaves. Some leaves may need a lot of hammering to give up their color.)
- Remove the wax paper and carefully peel away the tape and leaves—the imprint of the leaves will be left on the cloth.
- Now arrange new leaves, vines, and stems on your big piece of cloth. You can use the leaves as shapes and the stems and vines as lines to create a picture or pattern.
- Repeat the hammering process above.

Spinach Ink

What you are making:

Something special written in green ink

Materials:

- words
- a pencil or pen
- white paper
- green ink (Make from concentrated natural dye. Follow green dye directions on pages 34–35, but use less water. The ink shown here was made from one cup of water used to cook one and a half pounds of fresh spinach.)
- an artist's tipped pen (You can find one at an art or office supply store. A Speedball-type tipped pen with a broad nib works best: C-3, for example. If you want to be a nature purist, use the tip of a feather. It may be tougher to write with, though.)

How to do it:

- Use your pencil or regular pen to write your words on scrap paper; you will copy them over later.

- Dip artist's tipped pen into ink. You may want to practice writing on scrap paper.
- Copy your words in green ink onto a clean piece of paper.

Purple

Purple in nature can be unusual and mysterious. It is the color of things that are often hard to find: tropical fish and birds, rare orchids and butterflies. Purple is most commonly found in flowers. In fact, many shades of purple have flower names, such as lilac, lavender, violet, orchid, and hyacinth. A few fruits and vegetables are purple. So are distant mountains and the sky at twilight.

You probably don't think of purple clothes as anything unusual, but you would if you had lived two hundred years ago. The plants and other ingredients needed to make purple dye were very hard to find in nature, so they were very expensive. Only very rich people could afford purple-dyed clothing, and in some places it was actually against the law for anyone but the royal family to wear it. Because of this history, people have come to think of purple as the color of power and importance.

Purple is actually a mixture of red and blue. It shares some of the meanings of these two colors. Like red, it can be attention-getting. Like blue, it can seem dreamy. But purple has a special mysteriousness that we see in violet skies and faraway purple mountains.

Dried or Pressed Purple Flowers

If purple is as special to you as it is to many people, you may want to make something lasting with it—preserved flowers or a bookmark.

These dried violets are grayish white. They used to be deep violet. When they were dried in sand, they changed color. Yet other varieties of violets kept their color. Be prepared for surprises as you work with nature's colors!

What you are making:
Purple flowers preserved by drying

Materials:
- purple or violet flowers
- a sturdy box or bucket or other container
- sand from a playground sandbox or garden store
- time (It will take between one week and one month for the flowers to dry—see below.)

How to do it:
- Fill about three-quarters of the container with dry sand. (Flowers, especially wild-flowers, wilt quickly, so gather just before using.)
- Lay flowers on top of the sand. They should not be damp or wet.
- Cover all parts of the flowers with at least one more inch of sand.
- Leave for at least one week and up to a month. (Small flowers, like those shown here, take one week. Larger flowers, such as irises, need about one month.)
- Gently brush the top layer of sand away and shake any remaining grains off your dried flowers.

More on preserving flowers:
Another way to preserve flowers for use in art projects is by pressing them. You can press flowers by placing them between sheets of wax paper and putting them under a heavy pile of books for one week. Obviously, pressed flowers will be flat, while dried flowers are three-dimensional. Choose which will work best in your particular project.

Some flowers look best dried and others pressed; you can tell only by experimenting. Also, some flowers dry better in a mixture of borax (1 cup) and cornmeal (2 cups).

A Bookmark

What you are making:
A bookmark

Materials:
- several dried or pressed purple flowers (See instructions for drying or pressing on previous page.)
- a small piece of white cloth (muslin works well)
- scissors
- glue
- a small piece of clear plastic contact paper
- deep purple petunias or fresh blackberries for smudging (optional)

How to do it:
- Select dried or pressed flowers.
- Arrange flowers on cloth; consider your design carefully. Lightly glue flowers in place.
- Cut cloth to bookmark size, about 2 inches by 8 inches.

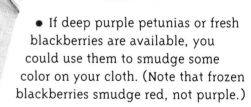

- If deep purple petunias or fresh blackberries are available, you could use them to smudge some color on your cloth. (Note that frozen blackberries smudge red, not purple.)
- Cut a piece of clear contact paper just a bit larger than the bookmark.
- Peel off backing and lay carefully over bookmark.
- Cut a second piece of contact paper, again just a bit larger than your bookmark. Peel and stick it to the back of your bookmark. Your bookmark is now covered in clear plastic. Trim the edges and enjoy.

Orange and Brown

O range brightens dull autumn days. There are many orange vegetables, such as pumpkins, that ripen in the fall. Leaves also turn orange (and red and yellow) as the temperatures become colder.

Leaves are green in spring and summer because of a pigment (a chemical inside the plant that works like paint) called chlorophyll. In autumn, the chlorophyll stops working, and other pigments that were in the leaves, but not as strong, get to show their colors. Weeds, garden plants, bushes, and trees turn shades of orange, brown, yellow, and red.

Orange is actually a mixture of red and yellow, and like yellow it is a warm, cheerful color. It is a color of the autumn holidays, Halloween and Thanksgiving. It is not popular with everyone, though. Some people think orange is so bright that it's tacky.

Brown is really a darkened, muddy orange. It is called an earth tone because brown is, after all, the color of the soil. Many creatures are brown: birds, insects, reptiles, and mammals. Brown is a good color for blending in and staying hidden. While fruits and vegetables are usually brightly colored to attract animals, the seeds inside them are often brown. Their color prevents them from being noticed by hungry creatures as the seeds rest in the soil, waiting to grow.

Because the plants we eat grow out of the brown earth and many favorite foods are shades of brown—bread, cookies, chocolate— brown is often seen as a homey, satisfying color. But some people find it dull, too.

A Warm Orange Tie-Dye

You can brighten up your wardrobe or room with an orange tie-dyed bandanna.

What you are making:

An orange tie-dyed cloth to use as a table mat or a bandanna

Materials:

- 24" x 24" square of unbleached muslin
- several rubber bands
- orange natural dye (see pages 34–35)
- a large glass jar or pot with a lid
- sunshine or a stove

How to do it:

- Make orange dye. (See pages 34–35. The material pictured on this page was dyed with orange made from a blend of red dye, made from beets, and yellow dye, made from turmeric.)

- Fold the square of cloth into a small size and tie with rubber bands. (You may want to experiment with different ways of folding and tying. You can fold into a square, triangle, or rectangle.)

- Pour dye into the large glass jar. This is a step in the sun-heating method, which takes longer. If you prefer quick results, see directions for the stove method below.

- Drop cloth into vegetable dye.

- Cover jar and let it heat in the sun for one day.

- Remove cloth from jar and unwrap. Rinse in clean water and lay out flat on newspapers to dry. You can iron when completely dry.

Stove method: For faster results, heat your cloth in a potful of dye. Have a grown-up help. Simmer cloth on the stove for 30 minutes, never allowing dye to boil. Let cool. Remove cloth from dye and unwrap to dry.

A Brown Weed Collage

What you are making:
A dried-weed collage to put on your wall

Materials:
- dried plants picked in middle or late fall

- paper (Heavy paper, such as construction paper, is preferred. White is probably best to show off ranges of color; orange would also look good.)

- brown construction paper (optional)

- white or clear glue (glue stick will not hold plants as well as wet glue)

How to do it:
- Gather a variety of weeds and other plants on a dry day. (These can be found in a garden, park, or along the roadside. Dried plants sometimes drop seeds and pieces, so keep them in a bag. Notice and collect a wide variety of color tones and textures.)

- Arrange the plants on paper. (You could create either a picture or an abstract design. If you are making a picture, you could use the brown construction paper to cut out objects, such as a house or fence or tree, to add to your scene.)

- Glue plants in place. Allow to dry thoroughly before hanging up.

For more fun: Since brown and orange are related colors, you might like the effect of adding a few orange leaves or dried orange flowers to your collage. Chrysanthemums are fall flowers that dry well. Alternately, you could combine tall dried weeds and flowers in a vase as a seasonal flower arrangement that would look particularly good on the Thanksgiving table.

Black, White, and Gray

Though they may not be our favorite colors, black and white are important in nature. Recognizing them is a matter of life and death for animals. In the white of daylight, many creatures must know to wake and search for food or a mate. In the blackness of night, they must take their vital rest.

Animal fur is often black or white (or both). Black is also the color of birds, black-berries, and many bugs. There are white birds, flowers, seashells, and clouds.

Black and white have the most powerful meanings of all the colors. Black, the color of rocks, means strength and seriousness. Judges wear black robes. Because it is the color of night or darkness, black reminds many people of the unknown and of death. Black is the color of funerals.

If black is the unknown, white is the color of knowledge, of things lit up so you can see them. It is the color of cleanliness and purity and is used in religious ceremonies such as marriages. Yet white can also seem so light, like dandelion fuzz, that it is undependable and so cold, like snow, that it's uncaring.

Gray is a mixture of black and white. We see it in stones, animal fur, tree trunks, and pussy willows. Like white, it can mean knowledge. People call a brain "gray matter." And like black, gray is solid and serious. Of course, some people just find it boring.

A Black-and-White Picture

Use the colors with the strongest contrast and meanings to make some very dramatic art.

What you are making:
A white-on-black picture

Materials:
- several hard-boiled eggs (Ask an adult to boil them for you.)
- a pencil
- a piece of black construction paper
- glue

How to do it:
- Peel the hard-boiled eggs, breaking the shells into small pieces.
- Draw a design or picture with a pencil on the black paper. Drip glue onto the design.
- Drop the eggshells on the paper, covering the glued area. (Experiment with the amount of eggshell you drop. You can add thick or thin layers of shell.)
- Let the picture dry for a few minutes.
- Pick up the paper and tilt it so the excess shell pieces fall off.
- Let the picture dry thoroughly.

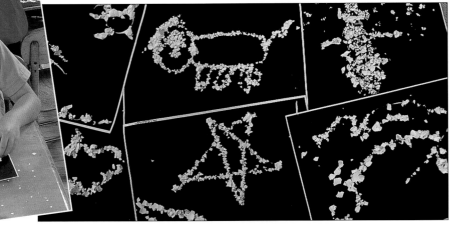

Drawing in Black and Gray

What you are making:
A drawing

Materials:

- masking tape

- charcoal (Get a piece of burned wood from a fireplace. Be sure it has cooled off completely first!)

- white paper

- ashes from a cold fire (optional)

How to do it:

- Wrap masking tape around the end of the piece of charcoal. This is where you will hold it—handling charcoal can be messy!

- Now your charcoal is ready to draw with. You can use the rough, smooth, thin, or thick edges of your piece to create different kinds of lines and textures on your paper.

- Use your finger to smudge the drawing, creating spots or thick lines.

- If you want to add gray, dip your finger in the ashes and smear them on your picture. (This can be very messy!)

- To seal the colors on your drawing, spray it with non-aerosol hair spray. Let dry.

For more fun:

Charcoal can also be the basis for black paint. Place charcoal in an old metal bowl or other round container that you don't plan to use again for food. Use a smooth, fist-sized rock to crush the charcoal into a powder. Mix a small amount of water, a few drops at a time, into the powder until you get a paintlike consistency.

Drawing from nature: Artists have used charcoal for drawing and painting for centuries. In fact, when you draw or write, you often use art supplies that come from nature. Your pencil is made of lead, a natural substance; chalk is really soft rock; and India ink, often used by artists, is made from the burned soot of certain woods or the soot of burned tar, pitch, and bones.

Multicolored Art

After making projects in just one color, you may be itching to create art with many colors. There is an easy way to get a variety of colors from one source—a head of red cabbage—with the help of a few kitchen ingredients.

What you are making:
Pictures with many colors dripped onto them

Materials:
- a head of red cabbage
- a stainless-steel pot
- 4 cups of water
- a stove (and a grown-up to help you use it)
- a liquid measuring cup or pitcher
- 4 small cups or jars
- vinegar
- liquid soap
- ammonia (or window-cleaning liquid with ammonia added)
- a paintbrush and an eye-dropper (You can find the latter at a drugstore.)
- different kinds of absorbent paper, including coffee filters, thin paper plates, drawing paper, paper towels, etc.

How to do it:
- Peel leaves off cabbage head. Put the leaves in the steel pot. Add 4 cups of water and cover.
- Simmer on the stove for about one hour. Do not use high heat or bring to a boil.
- Allow to cool.
- Strain liquid into a large measuring cup or pitcher. (You can throw away the cabbage leaves.)
- Set out 4 small cups or jars.
- Pour cabbage water from measuring cup into the small cups.
- Add a teaspoon of vinegar to one to make red.
- Add a teaspoon of liquid soap to another to make purple.
- Add a teaspoon of ammonia to a third to make green. Ammonia is very strong. Ask an adult for help with this step.
- Leave the fourth alone. It should be a nice shade of blue.
- Now you're ready to make art with your colors. These are dyes, not paints, so they are watery and different to use.

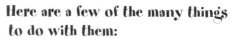

Here are a few of the many things to do with them:

- Try dripping dyes on paper towels or coffee filters with an eye-dropper to create abstract designs or pictures. You might choose to draw part of your picture with a marker, pencil, or pen and then add the colors later.

- You could also use the dyes to make a leaf print. Coat the back of a leaf (where the ridges are) with the dye. Gently lay a piece of paper down on the wet side and hold it firmly in place for about five seconds. (Don't slide the paper back and forth unless you want a blurred effect.)

- Use the dyes on regular drawing paper. They will not soak in as they do into paper towels.

They will stay on the surface at first, so you can streak them with a brush or smudge them with your finger or a paper towel. You get a nice effect, too, by dotting blobs or pulling long streaky lines across the paper with the eyedropper. Just don't move the paper until it's completely dry, or your picture will change!

- Your cabbage-water dyes, or some of the dyes listed on pages 34–35, can be used to color eggs. Be careful if you add vinegar. It helps the color stick to the egg but may affect the shade.

An extra color: You can make a very bright shade of blue by simmering leaves of a red cabbage in four cups of water in an *iron* pot. Simmer on the stove for one hour and then let stand overnight. When you wake up, you'll find a bright blue dye in your pot.

Make instant color with flowers. A very few special flowers can be rubbed directly onto paper to make art. This picture was made by drawing in pencil, then smearing portulaca blossoms for color. Portulaca is an annual that can be grown from seed or bought in garden stores in the spring. Certain crocus flowers will also smear color, as will deep purple petunias.

Making Dyes from Nature

You can make your own natural dyes—concentrated colors often used for staining cloth—from plants that grow in the wild or the garden. You can also find ingredients at the grocery store.

Warnings: Dye making must be done with adult supervision because it involves using a knife and stove.

Do not drink dyes, even when made with food.

When making and using dyes, be sure to cover kitchen countertops with newspapers. Dyes can stain!

Do not inhale the steam from your simmering dyes.

Wooden utensils may become stained if used to stir or remove items from dye.

Dyes are like foods: They will go bad if not used within a week of making. If your dye changes smell, throw it out. However, many dyes can be used later if frozen while fresh.

Before you get started: Next to each color name is a list of many ingredients that can be used alone to make a dye of that color. The quantities are the approximate amount needed to make one pint of dye. You should experiment to get the exact color results you want. Each ingredient is also followed by a code that tells you the best method to use to make the dye. Directions for each method are given on the next page. Method codes are the following:

H for Heating Method

S for Soaking Method

ST for Straight Method

COLORS

Red. Fresh beets (**S**, 5–8; use beets, skins, and tops); fresh or frozen cherries or strawberries (**H**, 2 cups); cranberries (**H**, 2 cups); honeysuckle berries (**H**, 2 cups); frozen concentrate of cranberry or boysenberry juice (**ST**, 2 cans)

Yellow. Turmeric (**ST**, 4 tablespoons in 2 cups hot water. You can find it in the spice section of your grocery store); goldenrod or marigold flowers (**H**, one loosely packed potful, includes flowers and stems); yellow onion skins (**H**, one loosely packed potful. Ask grocery-store manager for leftover skins in vegetable bins.)

Blue. Red cabbage (**H**, one-half head in iron pot); Concord grapes (**H**, 1 cup in iron pot)

Green. Fresh or frozen spinach (**H**, 2 lbs.); one loosely packed potful of any of the following: carrot tops, moss, lily-of-the-valley stalk and leaves, morning glory (**H**); dye blend of blue and yellow: red-cabbage and turmeric dyes

Orange. Red onion skins (**H**, one loosely packed potful. Ask grocery-store manager for leftover skins in vegetable bins); cosmos diablo (**H**, garden flower, one loosely packed potful of flowers and stems); coreopsis (**H**, garden flower, 25 or more flowers); dye blends of red and yellow: dye made from turmeric and beets *or* dye from turmeric with cranberry juice

Brown. Walnut shells (**H**, 1 dozen, boil 1 hour); strong tea (**ST**); strong coffee (**ST**)

Purple. Oregon or Concord grape skins (**H**, 1/2 cup); fresh or frozen blackberries or purple mulberries (**H**, 1 cup); red geranium leaves (**H**, 1 cup leaves in iron pot); dye blend of blue and red: red-cabbage dye with boysenberry concentrate (available at some grocery stores)

Black. Charcoal from campfire or fireplace (makes paint, not dye, if charcoal is crushed and mixed with water or egg yolk)

General directions for making one pint of dye:

- Chop or shred plant ingredient into small pieces
- Next, use either heating (**H**), soaking (**S**), or straight (**ST**) method, as indicated, to make dye.

Heating Method (**H**)

- Put plant material in pot.
- Add enough water to cover plant material, about 2 to 3 cups
- Simmer on stove for at least 30 minutes. Do not bring to a boil.
- Remove from heat.
- Let stand overnight.
- Strain liquid into a jar and store in refrigerator or freezer until ready to use.

Soaking Method (**S**)

- Put plant material in a container that has a cover.
- Add enough water to cover the plant material, about 2 to 3 cups.
- Cover and refrigerate overnight or up to a week, depending on the plant material.
- Strain liquid into a jar and store in refrigerator or freezer until ready to use.

Straight Method (**ST**)

- Liquids such as juices, tea, or coffee can be used as is.

Using dye on yarn or cloth:

- Heat or reheat dye to simmering point.
- Add 2 tablespoons of vinegar per pint of dye. (Vinegar will keep the dye from fading with wash and wear but may affect the color.)
- Put your yarn or cloth in the dye and let it simmer until it is slightly darker than desired. Let cool.
- Remove yarn or cloth from dye and rinse in cold water until water runs clear.
- Lay out to dry. Ironing will help the dye "set."

Using dye to make paint:

- Add 1 teaspoon cornstarch to a small amount of dye. (Amount used depends on the quantity and color desired.)
- Gently simmer on stove, stirring constantly, until white cornstarch turns clear and the color darkens.

More about dyes:

Cloth dyed in natural dyes can be washed occasionally, but frequent washing will wash the dye away. A chemical called a mordant is usually added to dyes to prevent fading. Many mordants are unsafe for children to use. However, a mordant called alum is relatively safe and can be bought in drugstores or large grocery stores.

A Brief History of Color Use

No one knows exactly how long ago people started making and using color. The oldest-known colored object is a piece of dyed cloth. It was placed in a tomb more than 5,000 years ago. (The use of color is probably even older, though.) Around the time that cloth was created, people also used colors from nature to paint their bodies and make pictures on the walls of caves. And they began to color things they used every day: their dishes, the baskets they used to gather food, and more. Through the years many items came to be colored with dye, including clothing, rugs, artwork, art supplies, printing inks, cosmetics, and even foods.

Over the centuries, people have discovered many natural color producers: plants, rocks, soil, and even insects and snails. For example, people eventually figured out that the best red came from an unusual source. They discovered tiny bugs in Central and South America called cochineal insects that could be scraped off prickly pear cacti, then heated, dried, and ground into a red powder. The powder would be mixed with water and other ingredients to make a dye that stained yarn or cloth bright red.

In Asia, printmaking and decorating pots with colored glazes, or mixtures of minerals, became high art forms.

Making dyes from nature sometimes took a lot of work. Imagine how much time it took to scrape thousands of cochineal insects from prickly pear cacti just to make one big pot, or vat, of dye.

All that work meant that early dyes tended to be expensive to buy. Some dyes were particularly expensive because they were made from plants that grew only in certain areas. The best blue dye, for example, came from the indigo plant, which grew in

India. It took a lot of time and money to make indigo and ship it to the rest of the world. Underground vats containing tons of water, indigo plant parts, and a few other ingredients (including urine) had to sit and ferment, like wine. When the dye was finally ready, it would still be many months before it reached customers, by ship, in Europe, the Americas, and other places. Unless you lived in India, you had to be pretty rich to afford bright blue clothing, rugs, and other items.

The brightest-colored dyes came from plants and materials found in hot, tropical places. The people in these areas tended to dress and decorate their homes in bright colors because they were readily available to them. In places where it was colder, such as Europe, homegrown dyes tended to make just muddy shades of green, yellow, and brown. If Europeans wanted bright colors, they had to pay for imported dyes and dye materials.

Peddlers traveled from place to place, selling dyes and raw materials. Those who knew how to make certain special dyes—usually groups of craftsmen—carefully guarded their valuable recipes. In some places a craftsman could be put to death for sharing his secrets with outsiders.

By the late 1800s, there were about one thousand different natural dyes in use.

These tiny bugs (above), called cochineal insects, are heated, dried, and ground into a red powder (at left), then used for dyeing cloth.

Then there was an accident that changed the history of dye making. In 1856, an eighteen-year-old chemistry student named William Henry Perkins, while trying to make a medicine, instead created a purplish liquid that he realized worked as an excellent dye. This discovery began the big business of making chemical dyes. More colors could be created from chemical dyes than natural dyes, and the synthetic dyes were cheaper and easier to produce. Large-scale production of natural dyes stopped.

But natural colors have not disappeared. In certain parts of the world, particularly Asia, interest in natural dyes never lessened. Good Turkish rugs made with natural dyes cost many thousands of dollars. The Turkish craftsmen who make them are very important people in their communities.

There is new interest in natural colors today. Many weavers and quilt makers prefer natural dyes, because they find that the colors they create are mellower and softer, and sometimes last longer than chemical dyes. And natural dyes, which don't always stain evenly, can create interesting patterns. Colors from natural dyes are like the colors in nature—unpredictable and beautiful, and they have a fascinating history.

More About Color

So what is color? You probably learned to name the colors before you went to school. Red apple, blue sky, yellow sun—it was easy then. But now you might want to know *why* the sky is blue or *why* apples are red. First you need to know a bit about light.

We see color because of the light that comes from the sun. This white light is made up of six main colors: red, yellow, blue (the primary colors); and orange, green, and violet (the secondary colors). You can see this when a ray of light is bent, or refracted, by moisture in the sky and a

rainbow forms. The primary and secondary colors, along with black and white, combine with one another to make *all* the different colors our eyes can see. (Scientists say that's over seven million colors!)

Why is the sky blue? The sky, like many other things in nature, doesn't really have a color of its own. It appears a certain color because of the way light breaks up and bounces off it and into our eyes. High in the sky, there are many tiny particles of dust and water. They act, in a way, like many tiny prisms. The colors in daylight pass through the particles—except for the color blue, which bounces off them and into our eyes, making us see blue.

Why are apples red? We say that apples and many other objects "have color" because they have chemicals in them called pigments. When daylight strikes an apple, a red rose, or a house painted red, the colors that are in

the white light are all absorbed by the pigment *except* red. The red light bounces off the pigment and into our eyes. The difference between something with a pigment and something without, like the sky or water, is that a pigmented object, with light shining on it, will *always* look the specific color that the pigment reflects. The sky, as you know, can be blue or gray or sunset orange, depending on the way the light hits it and is reflected. There are many pigments, and they all have unique chemical structures that make them reflect certain colors of light.

Without light, can we see color? No. The absence of light means an absence of color. You can see colors disappear if you go outside at twilight. Watch as they fade to gray and then black. Actually, colors also change a bit during the day as light changes. When the sun is low in the sky at sunrise or sunset, everything will look a slightly different color than in the light of noon. You can see this effect yourself if you use a camera to take photographs of the same object at different times of day. (Don't use a flash on the camera, though, or the experiment won't work.)

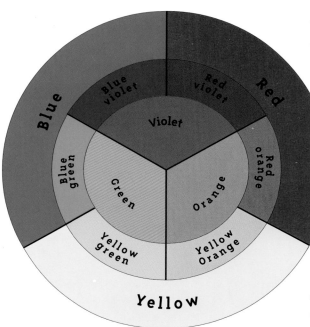

What are primary and secondary colors?

Red, blue, and yellow are the primary colors. They are colors that can be combined to make the secondary colors. All secondary colors are mixtures of two primary colors. Yellow and blue make green. Red and yellow make orange, and blue and red make violet. There are also six intermediate colors. They are made by mixing one of the primaries with one of the secondaries. They are blue violet, red violet, red orange, yellow orange, yellow green, and blue green. These are the twelve basic colors. You can see how they relate to each other on the color wheel above.

Why is violet a secondary color and not purple?

Purple is the name for *any* mixture of any red with any blue. (For example, pink, which is light red, with blue would make purple.) Violet is a combination of pure red and pure blue. It is violet that we see in a rainbow. Violet is the darkest of the primary and secondary colors.

If black and white aren't primary or secondary colors, what are they?

Black and white are two strong opposites, and they are called the neutral colors. Technically, white is the presence of all colors, and black is the absence of color. A pigment that *absorbs* all colors from light makes us see black. A pigment that *reflects* all colors makes us see white. These black and white pigments are often present in objects of other colors. A little black pigment makes a red leaf look darker, perhaps wine colored. A little white pigment makes a red flower look lighter or pink. Colors in nature are often not pure but contain bits of other colors.

What is brown?

Brown is not one of the twelve basic colors. You have to blend primaries, secondaries, intermediates, and/or neutrals to get brown and all the other colors. There are so many possible shades of brown because there are so many possible ways to make brown—by mixing all three primaries, for example, or mixing certain primaries with certain secondaries. In nature, colors that appear to be primary and secondary often have brown mixed into them. That is why they are often not as bright as the colors in your paint set. Colors with a lot of brown mixed in them are usually called earth tones.

Since white is all colors, can I mix the colors in my paint set and make white?

No. There are different ways to understand color. Color as light (what you see in a rainbow or prism) follows somewhat different rules than color as a solid (what you see when you mix paints together). I have described the way color behaves when it is light because that is what you see most often when you walk outside and look around—light in nature. (See the bibliography on page 40 for books you can read to learn more about the science of color.)

So now think again about color. How can you say what color something in nature really is? If a fruit—let's say a blueberry—is one color on the outside and another on the inside, which color is it really? What if it looks black on a stormy day but blue in bright sunlight? If it's one color when raw and another when cooked? Do you think anything in nature can always be the same color? There are many questions to ask and many experiments waiting to be done to discover the secrets of colors.

For my father.
For our camping trips together, for sun in green woods,
for twilight on the lake, for waking up to Nature...

Bibliography

Adrosko, Rita J. *Natural Dyes and Home Dyeing.* New York: Dover Publications, 1971.

Ardley, Neil. *Science Book of Color.* New York: Doubleday, 1996.

Cole, Alison. *Color.* New York: Dorling Kindersley Publishing, 1993.

Grae, Ida. *Nature's Colors: Dyes from Plants.* McMinnville, Oregon: Robin and Russ, Handweavers, 1991.

Kalman, Bobbie. *The Colors of Nature.* New York: Crabtree Publishing, 1993.

O'Neill, Mary. *Hailstone and Halibut Bones: Adventures in Color.* New York: Doubleday, 1989.

Varley, Helen, ed. *Color.* Los Angeles: The Knapp Press, 1980.

Acknowledgments

Many thanks to the kids and teachers from Yates Arts-in-Education School (especially Ava Scott) and Howe International Magnet School in Schenectady, New York, who did the projects and created the artwork from nature for this book. Special thanks to Betsy Neal, expert dye maker, weaver, teacher, and friend, who contributed so much knowledge and time. Special thanks to Susan Van Metre for detailed editorial work and a long-term commitment to this project. And, of course, thanks to four faithful, favorite models who've grown up along with this book: Steven S., Steven H., Laura, and Rachel.

CIP Data is available.
Published in the United States by Dutton Children's Books,
a division of Penguin Putnam Books for Young Readers
345 Hudson Street, New York, New York 10014
www.penguinputnam.com
Designed by Leah Kalotay
Printed in Hong Kong   First Edition
ISBN 0-525-46139-6   0 9 8 7 6 5 4 3 2 1